The Little House of Hope

TERRY CATASÚS JENNINGS

ILLUSTRATIONS BY
RAÚL COLÓN

NEAL PORTER BOOKS

HOLIDAY HOUSE / NEW YORK

A Note From the Author

This book was written in anger, but with pride. Anger at a realtor who told me he never rented to Hispanics because they lived four families to a house and always destroyed the properties where they lived. In 1961, when my family first came from Cuba to the United States, we lived in una casita. Three families lived there, twelve of us during the week and fourteen on weekends when my uncle's two sons came to stay with him. We came to the United States to regain our freedom, and in the case of my father, to avoid being jailed again. We landed with $50 for our family of four. In time we all became gainfully employed, each family finding a home of its own. And we all became citizens. From anger, I hope this book brings healing. It is dedicated with unwavering gratitude to the country that took us in, and to all immigrants who come to the United States in search of hope. —T.C.J.

In memory of Phil and Marty —R.C.

Neal Porter Books

Text copyright © 2022 by Terry Catasús Jennings
Illustrations copyright © 2022 by Raúl Colón
All Rights Reserved
HOLIDAY HOUSE is registered in the U.S. Patent and Trademark Office.
Printed and bound in January 2022 at Toppan Leefung, DongGuan, China.
The artwork for this book was created using watercolor and Prismacolor pencils on paper.
Book design by Jennifer Browne
www.holidayhouse.com
First Edition
1   3   5   7   9   10   8   6   4   2
Library of Congress Cataloging-in-Publication Data
Names: Jennings, Terry Catasús, author. | Colón, Raúl, illustrator.
Title: The little house of hope / by Terry Catasús Jennings ; illustrated
by Raul Colón.
Description: First edition. | New York : Holiday House, [2022] | "A Neal
Porter book." | Audience: Ages: 4 to 8 | Audience: Grades: K–1 |
Summary: "When Esperanza and her family arrive in the United States from
Cuba, they buy a little house, una casita. It may be small, but they
soon prove that there's room enough to share with a whole community"—
Provided by publisher.
Identifiers: LCCN 2021022870 | ISBN 9780823447169 (hardcover)
Subjects: LCSH: Cubans—United States—Juvenile literature. | Cuban
Americans—Juvenile literature. | Immigrants—United States—Juvenile
literature. | Immigrant families—United States—Juvenile literature.
Classification: LCC E184.C97 J46 2022 | DDC
973/.004687291—dc23/eng/20211014
LC record available at https://lccn.loc.gov/2021022870ISBN: 978-0-8234-4716-9 (hardcover)

ISBN 978-0-8234-4716-9 (hardcover)

It was a little house. Una casita.

When Esperanza and Manolo and Mami and Papi
came to the United States from Cuba,
they looked and looked
for a place where they could live
that didn't cost too much money.

And then they found it.

It was small.
It smelled like old, wet socks.
It had rickety, tattered furniture
from a church basement.

But even though they were far from home,
the family was together.
They were safe.
They were happy in la casita.

During the day, Papi painted other people's houses.
At night, he stocked shelves at a grocery store.

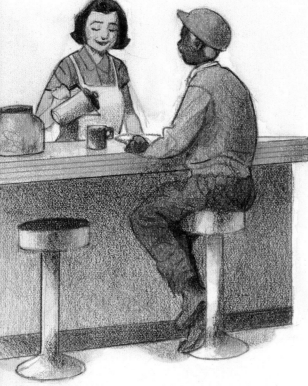

Mami worked at a laundromat
in the early mornings
and at a diner during the lunch shift.

Manolo and Esperanza
made their own breakfasts,
cafe con leche with buttered
toasts, and helped with
the chores at home.

They worked hard in school.
And everyone in the family began to learn English.

They came home to la casita
after work and after school
to the scrumptious smells of beans
and sofrito
and plantains—
the memories of home bubbling in Mami's pots.

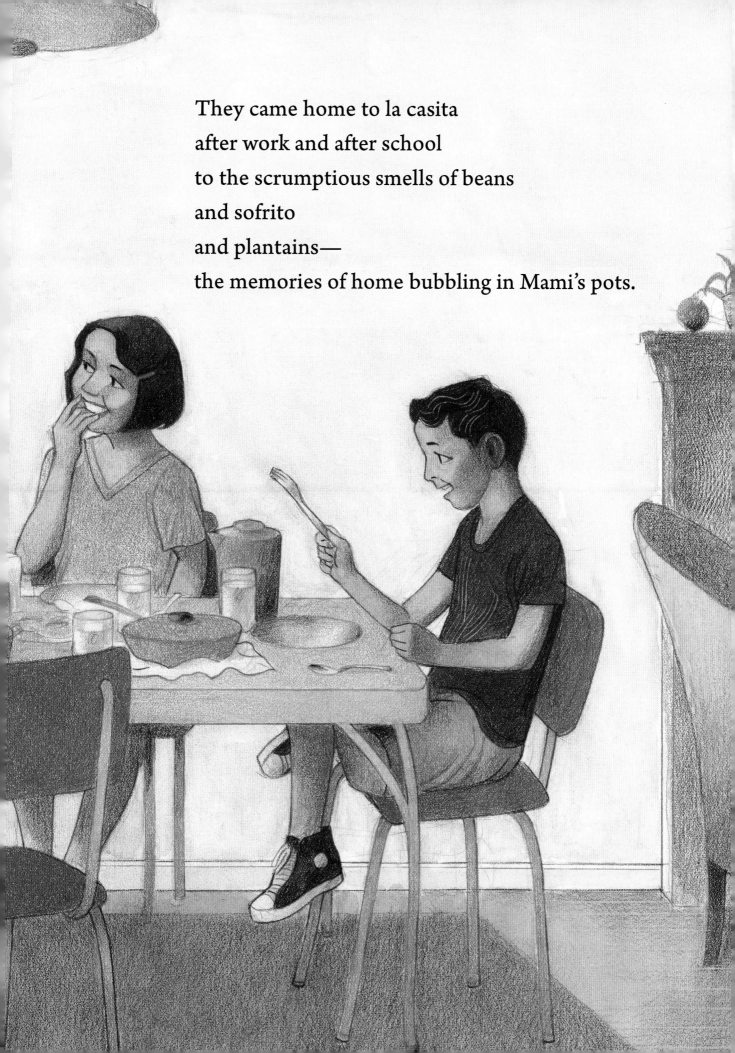

On weekends, they scrubbed and painted
and fixed anything that needed fixing.

When they were done,
Esperanza made a beautiful collage
with pictures of their home in Cuba.
On it she placed two words—
her name in Spanish and in English.
It was what they found in their new home.

In a few months, Mami's sister, Conchita,
joined them.
She came to live in la casita because
soldiers had taken her husband.
She was afraid to stay in Cuba, and she
and her baby Alina had no other place to go.

The family welcomed Conchita.
They made a room for her and Alina in the garage.
Esperanza helped take care of the baby,
and soon Conchita began taking care of
other people's children during the day.
She taught them songs in Spanish.
Their music and laughter filled la casita.

One day, a woman named Patricia came to look
for work at the diner where Mami cooked.
She and her husband Enrique and their two boys
had just come from Mexico.

They had ridden buses and trucks
and walked for miles
in search of a better life.

Mami invited them to la casita.

"There's room for two cots in the garage," Conchita said,
while changing diapers.

Manolo sighed. "I guess the boys can sleep in my room."

Mami agreed.

Esperanza started moving furniture.

By the time Papi came home, it was all settled.
Even though there wasn't much room,
everyone was happy in la casita.

Enrique used Papi's lawn mower to cut grass around
the neighborhood.
Soon he had his own mower, an old truck, and a trailer.
Manolo and the boys worked for him on weekends
and after school.

Soon Papi spoke English so well he got a job
as an accountant, like back home.

Mami got a job teaching Spanish
at the high school.

Conchita kept taking care of kids in la casita during the day.

And Patricia and her family got their papers
and found a home of their own.

Families came and
families went.

Esperanza was always the first to welcome them.
La casita offered a home for those who didn't
have a place to go.
It was a safe place, in a new land.

And whenever anyone left,
they left with a special present from Esperanza.